DEAR PEN PAL

PLEASE WRITE
ME A LETTER

Raffi Songs to Read

Like Me and

Illustrated by Lillian Ho

Words and music by Raffi and

YOU

Crown Publishers, Inc., New York

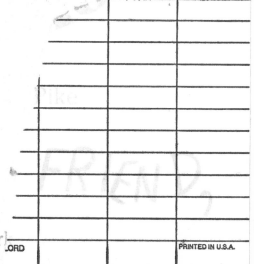

DATE DUE

Printed in the United States of America
http://www.randomhouse.com/

Library of Congress Cataloging-in-Publication Data
Raffi.
Like me and you / illustrated by Lillian Hoban.
p. cm. — (Raffi songs to read)
Summary: An illustrated version of Raffi's song about children all over the
world, who are much like one another despite living in different countries.
1. Children's songs—Texts. [1. Geography—Songs and music. 2. Songs.]
I. Hoban, Lillian, ill. II. Title. III. Series: Raffi. Raffi songs to read.
PZ8.3.R124Li   1994
782.42164'0268—dc20   93-9840
ISBN 0-517-59587-7 (trade)
0-517-59588-5 (lib. bdg.)
0-517-88552-2 (pbk.)

First paperback edition: August 1996
10 9 8 7 6 5 4 3 2 1

Front cover photograph © David Street
Back cover photograph © Patrick Harbron

 Printed on recycled paper

Janet lives in England,

Pierre lives in France,

Bonnie lives in Canada.

Ahmed lives in Egypt,

Moshe lives in Israel,

Bruce lives in Australia.

Ching lives in China,

Olga lives in Russia,

Ingrid lives in Germany.

Gita lives in India,

Pablo lives in Spain,

José lives in Colombia.

DEAR PEN PAL

DEAR PEN PAL:
I LIKE YOUR
LETTER
PLEASE SEND ME
A PICTURE
OF YOU

PIERRE
FRANCE

DEAR INGRID:
I LIKE

DEAR BONNIE:
I LIKE YOUR
LETTER
I LIKE SNOW
YOUR FRIEND
AHMED

MOSHE
ISRAEL

INGRID
GERMANY

And each one is much like another.

AHMED
EGYPT

TO GET LETTERS
YOUR PEN
PAL

PABLO
SPAIN

ENGLAND

DEAR BRUCE:
THANK YOU FOR
THE PICTURES
THERE ARE NO
SHEEP WHERE I
LIVE YOUR FRIEND
CHING

OLGA
RUSSIA

DEAR PEN PAL
THE KIDS IN
SCHOOL LIKE
TO WRITE
TO OTHER
KIDS

JOSE
COLOMBIA

YOUR
FRIEND,

BRUCE
AUSTRALIA

A child of a mother and a father.

A very special son or daughter.

A lot like me and you.

Koji lives in Japan,

Nina lives in Chile,

Farida lives in Pakistan.

Zosia lives in Poland,

Manual lives in Brazil,

Maria lives in Italy.

Kofi lives in Ghana,

Rahim lives in Iran,

Rosa lives in Paraguay.

Meja lives in Kenya,

Demetri lives in Greece,

Sue lives in America.

And each one is much like another.

A child of a mother and a father.

A very special son or daughter.

A lot like me and you.

Like Me and You

Words & music by Raffi, Debi Pike

Moderately, with feeling

1. Jan - et lives in Eng - land, Pierre lives in France, Bonnie lives in Can - a - da.

Ah-med lives in E - gypt, Mo - she lives in Is-ra-el, Bruce lives in Aus-tra-li-a.

Ching lives in Chi - na, Ol - ga lives in Rus - sia,

In-grid lives in Ger - man-y. Gi - ta lives in In - di - a, Pab-lo lives in Spain, Jo -

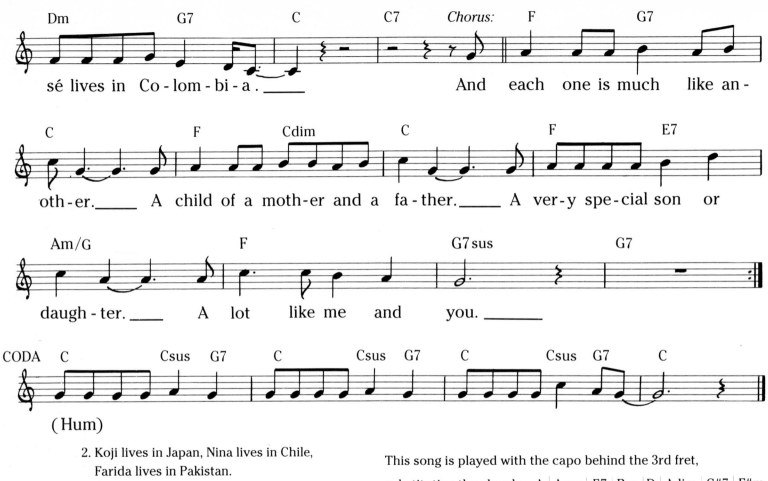

sé lives in Co-lom-bi-a.____ And each one is much like an-oth-er.____ A child of a moth-er and a fa-ther.____ A ver-y spe-cial son or daugh-ter.____ A lot like me and you._____

CODA

(Hum)

2. Koji lives in Japan, Nina lives in Chile,
Farida lives in Pakistan.
Zosia lives in Poland, Manual lives in Brazil,
Maria lives in Italy.
Kofi lives in Ghana, Rahim lives in Iran,
Rosa lives in Paraguay.
Meja lives in Kenya, Demetri lives in Greece,
Sue lives in America.

Repeat chorus

This song is played with the capo behind the 3rd fret,

substituting the chords

A	Asus	E7	Bm	D	Adim	C#7	F#m
C	Csus	G7	Dm	F	Cdim	E7	Am

for

Triangle